S0-BUC-637

"Come on, slug! You'll never catch me!" you shout to Jabba the Hutt, who is chasing you through the corridors of his palace.

In his thunderous voice, Jabba calls for guards to help capture you, but the guards must be busy elsewhere because no one responds. The corridor turns left, and you follow it around and around. You and Lando have been pretending to be Jabba's guards for days now, but you still don't know the palace very well. It's pretty confusing.

Suddenly you round another corner and find your way blocked by a group of palace guards. You stop so fast you nearly fall over. You are about to turn and run the other way when a deep voice growls, "Don't make a move."

You look up and see battered green armor. It's Boba Fett. His weapon is pointed right at you.

CHOOSE YOUR OWN STAR WARS® ADVENTURE®

RETURN OF THE JEDI

BY CHRISTOPHER GOLDEN

Illustrated by Phil Franké

BANTAM BOOKS

NEW YORK • TORONTO • LONDON • SYDNEY • AUCKLAND

RL 5.0

RETURN OF THE JEDI

A Bantam Skylark Book / September 1998

*Skylark Books is a registered trademark of Bantam Books, a division of
Bantam Doubleday Dell Publishing Group, Inc.
Registered in U.S. Patent and Trademark Office and elsewhere.*

*CHOOSE YOUR OWN ADVENTURE® is a registered trademark of Bantam Books,
a division of Bantam Doubleday Dell Publishing Group, Inc.
Registered in U.S. Patent and Trademark Office and elsewhere.*

*Original conception of Edward Packard
Interior illustrations by Phil Franké*

*All rights reserved.
®, ™, & © 1998 by Lucasfilm Ltd.
Cover art copyright © 1998 by Lucasfilm Ltd.
Illustrations copyright © 1998 by Bantam Doubleday Dell Books for Young Readers.*

*No part of this book may be reproduced or transmitted in any form or by any means, electronic
or mechanical, including photocopying, recording, or by any information storage and retrieval
system, without permission in writing from the publisher.
For information address: Bantam Doubleday Dell Books for Young Readers.*

*If you purchased this book without a cover you should be aware that this book is
stolen property. It was reported as "unsold and destroyed" to the publisher, and nei-
ther the author nor the publisher has received any payment for this "stripped book."*

ISBN 0-553-48653-5

Published simultaneously in the United States and Canada

Bantam Books are published by Bantam Books, a division of Bantam Doubleday
Dell Publishing Group, Inc. Its trademark, consisting of the words "Bantam
Books" and the portrayal of a rooster, is Registered in U.S. Patent and Trademark
Office and in other countries. Marca Registrada. Bantam Books, 1540 Broadway,
New York, New York 10036.

PRINTED IN THE UNITED STATES OF AMERICA
OPM   0 9 8 7 6 5 4 3 2 1

THIS ONE'S FOR DIANA CAPRIOTTI, WHO WORKED AS HARD ON THIS AS I DID, AND WHOSE ENTHUSIASM, MORAL SUPPORT, AND ALL-AROUND GOOD HUMOR WERE INVALUABLE IN THE COMPLETION OF THIS BOOK.

I would like to gratefully acknowledge the support and contributions of my agent, Lori Perkins; the team at Bantam, especially Karen Meyers and Beverly Horowitz; Sue Rostoni at Lucasfilm; radio scribe Brian Daley; the Jedi Master George Lucas, and every person whose hard work went into making the original film; and of course, as always, my wonderful wife, Connie, who knows this stuff even better than I do, and my sons, Nicholas and Daniel, through whose eyes I see Lucas's vision anew time and again.

RETURN
OF THE JEDI

WARNING!!!

Do not read this book straight through from beginning to end. These pages contain many exciting galactic adventures you may have as you take your place in the Rebellion against the evil empire of Emperor Palpatine and his minion, Darth Vader. Will you fight with your friends Luke Skywalker, Princess Leia, and Han Solo, or will you turn to the dark side of the Force?

From time to time as you read along, you will have to make a choice. But beware—what looks like the right choice may lead you to hidden danger and unknown enemies. Because every decision you make for yourself will have immediate consequences for the lives of your closest friends.

You're caught in the middle of a battle between good and evil. Courage and honor can lead you to glorious victory, but the dark side of the Force offers unimaginable power. Will you be strong enough to make the right choices? Read on and find out.

Good luck!

You were born and raised on the planet Tatooine, a dustball where moisture farming is big business. But you and your best friend, Luke Skywalker, always wanted to be fighter pilots, not farmers.

Not so long ago, you and Luke joined the Rebellion in a fight against the evil Emperor and Darth Vader, a fallen Jedi Knight. You met amazing people like Ben Kenobi, an aging Jedi; Princess Leia, a young Rebel leader; Han Solo, an intergalactic smuggler; Han's first mate, the Wookiee Chewbacca; as well as a pair of droids called R2-D2 and C-3PO. With this band of Rebels, you and Luke helped lead the Rebellion to an important victory. Luke himself fired the blast that destroyed the Death Star, the Empire's most fearsome weapon. Through all of the incredible adventures, you have remained loyal to your friends and the struggle of good over evil.

However, the war is far from over. It now seems that Darth Vader—the most frightening man you've ever met—has a personal vendetta against Luke. Not long ago in Cloud City, you and your friends—along with an old friend of Solo's named Lando Calrissian—faced Darth Vader. This time, things didn't go your way.

TURN TO PAGE 7.

2

Han signals to Chewbacca, farther along the tree line. You pass along the instructions, but you and Leia go with Han. He sneaks up on the remaining guard from behind and taps him on the shoulder.

"Excuse me, pal," he says. "Is this where I sign up for the bunker tour?"

"Who?" the guard says, turning around. "Halt! Get your hands up!"

"No, I don't think so," Han replies, and walks away.

The guard follows him around the corner, right into a squad of Rebel commandoes. After the guard is captured, Han orders the commandoes to spread out, to prepare for the destruction of the shield generator, and to cover the door.

Unfortunately, before you and your friends can set the charges and blow the generator, more Imperial troops arrive with huge armored mechanical walkers. You're badly outnumbered. You've been captured.

Which is when the Ewoks attack!

The furry little creatures swoop out of the forest and fight the Imperial troops as fiercely as the Rebels themselves. Together, the Ewoks and commandoes ambush the stormtroopers from dozens of locations.

TURN TO PAGE 65.

"His plan is not going to work if he gets eaten by a rancor!" you snap. "Besides, you can just hang back and let me go after him. That way, even if I'm caught, your disguise is still intact. You can do the job by yourself as well as we could together."

Lando shakes his head. "I don't know about this, kid," he says. "Luke's plan was pretty specific. He obviously put a lot of thought into this before we came after Han. And he's from this planet, after all. He knows what he's doing."

"I'm from this planet, too!" you say, trying not to raise your voice. "I know how dangerous that rancor is! And Luke didn't know he'd have to face one when he walked in here. If he had, I think he might have had a different plan."

"If we blow it now," Lando says, "we might be condemning ourselves and Han and the others to death. Is that what you want?"

"Of course not," you reply.

IF YOU GO DOWN INTO THE PIT AFTER LUKE, TURN TO PAGE 96.

IF YOU STAY SILENT AND WAIT, TURN TO PAGE 100.

"Sorry, Lando," you say. "I'd never forgive myself if I didn't go along and watch over Luke."

"Welcome aboard, kid," Han says. "Guess I've got my crew."

A short time later, you board the stolen Imperial shuttle *Tydirium*. A squadron of Rebel commandoes boards in the rear. In front, you sit with Princess Leia and Luke behind Han and Chewbacca, with the droids in the rear of the cockpit. It's more than the ship was built to hold comfortably, but it feels right to you that the group is all together.

Han seems distracted until Leia taps him. "You awake?" she asks.

"Just looking at the *Falcon*," he says. "Can't shake the feeling I'm never gonna see her again."

Han pilots the shuttle through its launch, and then the ship makes the leap to hyperspace to appear sometime later not far from the moon of Endor. The new Death Star is in orbit around Endor, and everyone is upset by the sight of it. It is the most dangerous weapon ever devised. But it isn't completed yet—there is still time to stop the Empire from putting it to use if the Rebel fleet can destroy it. Which won't happen unless you can turn off the deflector shield.

TURN TO PAGE 11.

"We're sitting ducks here," you say. "We've got to move now!"

Leia grunts and holds her hand to her wounded shoulder.

"Leia? Can you make it?" you ask.

"You run," she replies. "Han will hold on to your shoulder, and I'll bring up the rear."

"No!" Han snaps. "We've got to wait for Lando and Chewie!"

"It's going to be a long wait, Solo," a voice says from around the corner.

You peer around and see Boba Fett. He and a whole group of Jabba's men have Lando at gunpoint.

"Surrender," Fett says, "or he dies."

"We surrender," you say immediately, without even consulting the others.

It's either that, or Lando will be killed. Silently, you vow revenge on Boba Fett. Without him, you might have escaped.

"Oh, my!" Threepio exclaims from where he stands next to Jabba.

Jabba only laughs from deep in his throat and begins to speak. Threepio translates Jabba's orders. The guards position you, Lando, Leia, and Han in front of the platform where Jabba's huge worm-body rests.

STAY COOL ON PAGE 12.

Vader captured Han Solo, froze him solid in a material called carbonite, and turned him over to a bounty hunter named Boba Fett. Now you and the rest of your friends have returned, after all this time, to your home planet of Tatooine, in order to save Han from the criminal mastermind Jabba the Hutt, who put the bounty on Han's head.

It has taken long days of planning, but finally you are ready for Han's rescue. You and Lando Calrissian have infiltrated Jabba's palace guards. Your Jedi powers were of some help in this—they have increased a bit, but not anywhere near as much as Luke's.

"I don't know how long we can fool them," you tell Lando, as you stand at attention in Jabba's Great Hall, staring at your coworkers—a nasty crew of alien pirates, bounty hunters, and guards. On one wall hangs the huge black block of carbonite inside which your friend Han Solo is frozen. You try not to look at it.

"The droids should be here soon. We just have to wait until tonight. We can get to Han then," Lando whispers back.

STAY UNDERCOVER ON PAGE 111.

"So much for your plan, Luke," Lando says. "Without the kid and me as guards on the skiff, we've lost our advantage."

"I'm not sure about that," you say. "I think I can get a blaster."

Luke's eyes widen. "If you can manage that, this might still work. Follow my lead."

A plank is extended above the pit. A guard unties Luke's hands just before he's forced out onto the plank. Luke walks out and pauses a moment. He signals to R2-D2, on board the sail barge, and jumps off the plank.

Instead of falling, Luke spins around, grabs hold of the plank, and bounces back up into the air. Meanwhile, Artoo has fired a bright metal object out of his body. It flips through the air and lands in Luke's hand—his lightsaber! Luke's first slash cuts your hands free. The four guards point their weapons at Luke, but you reach out with the Force, using every ounce of energy you have, and grab the blaster from the guard in front.

TURN TO PAGE 95.

The Emperor has your lightsaber as well as Luke's at his feet. With a single thought, you call your lightsaber to you and turn toward Luke.

"I'm sorry," you say, giving in to your fear for the Rebellion and your rage at the Emperor.

Luke looks shocked. He can't believe that you are doing this. But he calls his lightsaber and ignites it, turning to defend himself from your attack.

"No!" Luke cries. "Don't let him do this to you! Don't you see? Your sacrifice will be for nothing. The Rebellion will never survive unless the Emperor and this station are destroyed!"

But you feel the dark side sweeping over you now, and the power that the Emperor talked about surges through you. Suddenly you think about all the times that you were jealous of Luke because he was so good with the Force, because he was nearly a Jedi Master and you only a Jedi-in-training. You attack him and drive him back. Luke is not fighting at his best because he does not want to kill you.

"Do what you must," Luke says at last. "I cannot take your life."

TURN TO PAGE 33.

You follow Luke's lead and leap from the skiff to the barge. On the deck, Luke is fighting dozens of guards. You smash into the main cabin, where Leia is still trying to strangle Jabba with her chains. Just as you arrive, she succeeds. The Hutt stops moving.

"Got him!" Leia says, out of breath.

"Sure did," you agree. "Now let's get out of here."

You use your lightsaber to cut a huge hole in the main cabin wall.

Behind you, Jabba stirs. It could be nothing, but you want to make sure. Fortunately, he is lying on a platform with wheels under it. You and Leia push the platform to the hole in the wall, and Jabba tumbles out.

As if sensing the Hutt's falling body, the Sarlacc opens its mouth to catch Jabba—and Chewbacca is able to pull Han and Lando up a bit higher, out of the way. The Sarlacc swallows Jabba. Suddenly, the huge monster begins to choke on the Hutt's enormous body. You watch as the Sarlacc recedes into the pit and disappears. Without the Sarlacc pulling at the other end, Chewie is able to hoist Han and Lando to safety. Though you left them behind to help Leia, in the end you were able to save Han and Lando after all.

TURN TO PAGE 50.

As you wait for the Death Star traffic controller to allow you to land on Endor, Luke notices a huge Star Destroyer nearby.

"Vader's on that ship," he says. "I'm endangering the mission. I shouldn't have come."

But then the Death Star traffic controller announces that the shuttle is cleared to land on Endor. Luke still believes that Vader is on the Destroyer, but Han tells him Vader would never have let the shuttle through if he knew Luke was on board. You wonder, though, if Vader has some plan none of you has thought of yet.

Before long the shuttle has landed on Endor. The flight crew and commandoes gather in the forest on the moon's surface and begin to plan. It's a straight march through the woods to the building where the shield generator is housed. But you have to be careful not to let the Imperials know you're coming. Quietly, you and your friends make your way through the woods, with the commandoes following.

Chewbacca sniffs the air. Han holds up a hand to signal everyone to stop.

"What is it?" you whisper.

SOMETHING'S NOT RIGHT.

TURN TO PAGE 30.

"His Immensity, Jabba the Hutt, offers you poor Rebel prisoners a choice!" C-3PO announces happily. He honestly believes that Jabba is going to propose some kind of fair deal. But you know better. You've seen Jabba in action before.

"Jabba will allow you to choose between revealing all of your knowledge about the Rebellion," Threepio translates. "Or . . . oh dear! He will have you dropped into a pit with the rancor!

"Oh!" Threepio cries. "The horror!"

You know that whatever information you give to Jabba he will sell to the highest bidder. Which will probably be Darth Vader and the Empire. But still, you must decide.

IF YOU REFUSE TO TELL JABBA WHAT HE WANTS TO KNOW, TURN TO PAGE 39.

IF YOU DECIDE TO TELL JABBA WHAT HE WANTS TO KNOW, TURN TO PAGE 89.

"You two keep after that one," he shouts. "I'll take the two behind us."

Luke uses his retrothrusters to slow his bike, letting the new pursuers catch up with him. You and Leia surge ahead after the remaining speeder in front. The scout you're chasing weaves in and out of trees, obviously hoping you'll crash. Somehow Leia sticks with him.

"We've got to get him, Leia," you say. "We can't afford to let even one of these guys report back to their base."

"I'm working on it!" she snaps.

She guides the speeder bike through a pair of trees sideways. When you're right side up again, you see the speeder straight ahead.

"Now!" Leia shouts.

She fires and misses! The scout turns and fires his sidearm blaster back at you. Your speeder bike is hit, spinning out of control. Luckily, both of you leap from the bike a moment before it crashes. When you look up, you see that the scout has lost control of his speeder while looking back at you and Leia. He crashes into some trees, and his bike explodes.

Then you black out. When you come to, a short, furry creature is poking you with a spear.

OUCH! TURN TO PAGE 53.

With the shield down, the Rebel fleet in space above Endor is able to destroy the Death Star. The explosion in the sky is as bright as a second sun. The Ewoks and Rebels all cheer.

"I just hope Luke got off the Death Star in time," Han says.

"He did," Leia whispers. "I can sense it. He's coming back."

"Well, then, I guess we just have to hope Lando's okay, too," you say.

Luckily, Lando is fine. That night, a huge celebration is held on Endor for all the Rebel troops. Luke has laid out the armor of Darth Vader on a pyre and set it aflame. Later, you find him staring off into the darkness.

"What are you looking at, Luke?" you ask. "Is Ben back?"

He smiles. "Yes. And Yoda. And one other."

"Vader?" you ask, surprised.

"No." Luke shakes his head. "No longer Darth Vader, but the original—Anakin Skywalker. My father. They're here with us, old friend, and they'll never be far away. The balance has turned toward the good. The Jedi have returned."

THE END

Jabba laughs in his booming voice and responds. "Your Jedi mind powers will not work on me," Threepio translates.

"Nevertheless, Jabba," Luke says, "I'm taking Captain Solo and his friends. You can either profit by this . . . or be destroyed. But I warn you not to underestimate my powers."

Jabba is very still as he replies. Threepio translates: "There will be no bargain, young Jedi. I shall enjoy watching you die."

Jabba laughs heartily. You know what will probably come next—the rancor pit—and you wonder if you should warn Luke. It would take away one of Jabba's advantages and probably help bring a quick end to the fight. But Luke's plan is to keep you and Lando as a last resort. If you reveal yourselves now, you could blow that.

IF YOU KEEP SILENT, TURN TO PAGE 21.

IF YOU TRY TO WARN LUKE, TURN TO PAGE 74.

You are stunned. But perhaps that is what the power of the Force is all about. Love and forgiveness. You can feel the dark side retreating as Luke helps you to your feet.

Together, you return to the surface of Endor. The Death Star is destroyed, the Rebellion is victorious, and that night a huge celebration is hosted by the Ewok tribes. A large funeral pyre is built, and Darth Vader's armor is laid atop it before it bursts into flames.

A short time later, you come upon Luke staring into the darkness as fireworks light the sky above.

"What are you looking at, Luke?" you ask. "Is Ben back?"

He smiles. "Yes. And Yoda. And one other."

"Vader?" you ask, surprised.

"No." Luke shakes his head. "Not Darth Vader, but Anakin Skywalker. My father. They're here with us, old friend, and they'll never be far away. The balance has turned toward the good. The Jedi have returned."

THE END

You don't think you stand a chance in a battle against Jabba the Hutt. You turn and run down the corridor, trying to get your lightsaber out of your shirt.

But Jabba moves much faster than you ever expected. He is right behind you, his deep laugh bellowing from his mouth.

Finally, you get your lightsaber. It crackles to life in your hands. You spin, ready to slash the Hutt to death, if that's what it takes to escape.

But Jabba is too close. He smashes into you, and you lose your grip on your lightsaber. It flies from your hand and clatters to the floor. You scramble to reach it, but before you can move, Jabba flops on top of your legs, and you feel something crack.

Worse, Jabba has you trapped now. He lies on top of your legs, pinning you to the floor. The lightsaber is just out of your reach, and you can't concentrate enough to use the Force to draw it. All you can do is lie there as Jabba calls out to his guards.

When the guards arrive, they drag you off to the dungeon, where you find Lando. The two of you spend the rest of your days locked away, hoping that Luke and the others have escaped alive and will someday return to rescue you.

THE END

"The Emperor has been expecting you," Vader tells him.

"I know, Father," Luke replies.

"So, you have accepted the truth," Vader says.

"I've accepted the truth that you were once Anakin Skywalker, my father," Luke says.

You watch Vader for any reaction. He pauses a moment, as though Luke's words disturb him.

"That name no longer has any meaning for me," Vader says at last.

"It is the name of your true self," Luke insists. "You've only forgotten. I know there is good in you. The Emperor hasn't driven it from you fully. That was why you couldn't destroy me on Cloud City. That's why you won't bring me to your Emperor now. Come away with me, Father."

Vader pauses again. "Obi-Wan once thought as you do. You don't know the power of the dark side. I must obey my master."

"I will not turn, and you'll be compelled to kill me," Luke says defiantly.

"If that is your destiny," Vader replies.

A chill runs through your body. You see that Luke was wrong about his father. Vader is evil, through and through.

TURN TO PAGE 85.

With Luke's words, Jabba begins to laugh, his huge, disgusting belly swaying with every chuckle.

"With your wisdom, I'm sure that we can work out an arrangement which will be mutually beneficial and enable us to avoid any unpleasant confrontation," the holo of Luke continues.

You cringe. You know the part coming up is going to make C-3PO very unhappy, though it's all part of the plan.

"As a token of my goodwill," the holo goes on, "I present to you a gift: these two droids. Both are hardworking and will serve you well. I await your decision."

"What did he say?" Threepio cries. "This can't be! Artoo, you played the wrong message!"

Jabba only laughs harder and announces that he will not make a deal with Luke. But he *will* keep the droids.

So much for Plan A, you think as Artoo and Threepio are taken away. Good thing there's Plan B.

TURN TO PAGE 62.

You know that if you warn Luke, you will be giving away the only secret advantage he has. Luke is a Jedi Master, and you must have faith in his ability to overcome whatever Jabba can throw at him.

Threepio is obviously agitated, and the droid suddenly cries out to Luke, trying to warn him of the trapdoor in the floor. You are relieved that your cover is saved and Luke warned. Jabba bellows orders to his huge, piglike guards to take Luke away.

As the Gamorrean guards begin to move toward him, Luke reaches out with the Force. A blaster flies from the hand of one of the guards. As if pulled by some invisible rope, it lands in Luke's right hand. At the same moment, one of the guards grabs Luke around the chest and begins to crush him. Together they stumble onto the trapdoor.

Leia tries to shout a warning, but it's too late! The trapdoor opens, and Luke and the guard both fall into the rancor pit. You've got to help your friend. You take a step forward. Lando grabs your arm.

"Luke's plan . . ." he begins.

YOU HAVE TO SAY SOMETHING ON PAGE 4.

"Never," you say, purposely repeating the word Luke used.

"Well, then I have another use for you," the Emperor says. He turns to Luke. "Skywalker, perhaps the fate of the Rebellion is too . . . distant at the moment. Perhaps you need a crisis closer to home. For instance . . .

"Vader, you will kill the little Jedi now."

"Yes, my master," Darth Vader says.

He ignites his lightsaber and turns toward you.

"No!" you cry, and reach out with the Force for your own lightsaber, lying at the Emperor's feet.

You fight with Vader, but there is no way that you can beat him. He is second only to the Emperor in power. As a warrior, he is second to none. You have no chance.

At first, Luke will not even look at you. But you can see the horror, sadness, and fury in his face when he finally turns to you.

"Luke, don't!" you shout.

WHAT WILL HAPPEN NEXT ON PAGE 76?

During the feast, you notice that Luke, Han, and Leia are missing. You wonder where they could be, so you go looking for them. When you discover Han and Leia talking, you don't want to interrupt. But you don't see Luke anywhere.

You cough. Han and Leia finally see you.

"Bad timing, kid," Han says.

"Sorry," you say. "I just wanted to know where Luke is."

Leia drops her eyes. She won't look at you. Han looks upset, too. Suddenly you know.

"Vader," you say. "I could feel him here on Endor, but I never thought Luke would go to him."

Leia smiles a little. "You're a Jedi, too, aren't you?"

"I am," you answer. "But I don't know what to do now. I shouldn't let Luke face Vader alone. But you need me here. I wish Ben were here, or Yoda, to tell me what to do."

IF YOU STAY WITH THE OTHERS,
TURN TO PAGE 71.

IF YOU GO AFTER LUKE,
TURN TO PAGE 93.

24

You want to call out, to warn Luke, but you are bleeding badly and it is hard enough just to keep your eyes open.

"No!" Luke says again, turning toward Vader.

"Then you must watch your friends perish!" the Emperor says triumphantly.

"I won't let you kill them!" Luke shouts. He ignites his lightsaber.

"It's beyond your control now, Luke," Vader says.

As the two men move into battle, their lightsabers clashing noisily, you realize that there is a strange new tone in Darth Vader's voice. He sounds . . . sad.

"I have to stop him!" Luke declares.

"You will fail," Vader tells him.

Father and son fight on, and the Emperor smiles his cruel, evil smile, urging them on.

"That's it!" the Emperor says. "Use your anger, boy! Let the hate flow through you!"

Suddenly Luke just stops. He shuts off his lightsaber.

"No," he says. "This is wrong. I won't do it. I won't fight you, Father."

You smile weakly. Luke is in control now. Instead of fighting with hate and fear and anger, he has opened himself to the Force.

WAY TO GO, LUKE! TURN TO PAGE 38.

"No matter what you tell Jabba, he's never going to let us go," Han says.

You're tempted to believe him. He has had a lot of experience with Jabba over the years when he was a space pirate, before he joined the Rebel Alliance.

But you have to try to save yourselves. You can't just decide to die. You know you don't stand a chance inside the rancor's pit.

You begin to talk, answering every one of Jabba's questions. You tell him about the Rebellion's leaders and its bases. You reveal Luke's plan to free Han. You say that Luke would do anything to save your lives. You talk for hours, knowing the entire time that your friends hate you now, because they believe you've betrayed the Rebellion. It doesn't matter. All that matters is that you all will live.

When you've told Jabba everything he wants to know, the Hutt decides to take a nap. He mumbles one last thing to Threepio before sleeping.

"The generous Jabba has decided to alter his agreement with you," Threepio says. "Since only the Lieutenant helped Jabba with his questions, only the Lieutenant will be freed. The rest of you will spend your lives in Jabba's dungeons!"

THAT WASN'T SUPPOSED TO HAPPEN!

TURN TO PAGE 63.

Jabba and his followers gather aboard a much larger hover boat called a sail barge. Boba Fett is with Jabba, and so is Princess Leia, whom Jabba has decided to keep as a slave. You can see that C-3PO is on board the sail barge as well, as is R2-D2; Jabba has put him to work serving drinks to the guests.

But on the sand skiff, it's just you and Lando, Luke, Han, and Chewbacca—along with two other real guards. The skiff is almost at the Pit of Carkoon, a huge, sucking hole in the desert floor, inside which the terrible Sarlacc dwells.

One of the real guards extends a plank above the pit. Just before the second guard forces Luke onto the plank, Lando unties his hands. Luke walks out and pauses a moment. He signals to Artoo, on board the sail barge, and then jumps.

Instead of falling into the pit, Luke spins around, grabs hold of the plank, and bounces back up into the air. Meanwhile, Artoo has fired a bright metal object out of his body. It flips through the air and lands in Luke's hand—his lightsaber! The two guards point their weapons at Luke, but Lando hits one of them with a long staff, and you disarm the other with your lightsaber. The guards are your prisoners.

TURN TO PAGE 113.

But just as you manage to wiggle free, you hear heavy armored boots clomping down the hall toward you. As you stand to peer across Jabba's unmoving form, you see the battered green armor of Boba Fett. He and some of Jabba's Gamorrean guards have their weapons aimed at you. They have Lando captive as well.

"Not a move," Boba Fett warns.

"They've got us, kid," Lando says sadly. "Unless you've got a backup plan, I'd say we're in big trouble."

Unfortunately you don't have another plan. Boba Fett escorts both of you to a group of Hutts on a distant planet, where he collects a stash of money for bringing them Jabba's killer. You and Lando are kept as slaves. Every moment of every day, you wait for the time when the Hutts will let down their guard so you can escape. It's a terrible way to live, but you console yourself with the knowledge that the others are safe.

THE END

Luke looks at you, then stares out the window at the Rebel fleet approaching through space beyond the Death Star.

"Never," he says to the Emperor.

The Emperor laughs, then turns to you.

"And what of you, young Jedi?" the Emperor asks. "I told you you might be of use. Here is the moment. Will you turn to the dark side? Will you take the life of Luke Skywalker, your oldest and truest friend, if it means allowing the Rebellion to survive and do battle another day?"

You look at Luke. You know that even if the Emperor lets the Rebels go, with the new Death Star operational it will only be a matter of time before the Empire destroys the Rebellion entirely. But a small chance is better than no chance at all isn't it?

IF YOU TAKE UP YOUR LIGHTSABER AGAINST LUKE, TURN TO PAGE 9.

IF YOU REFUSE TO STRIKE YOUR FRIEND, TURN TO PAGE 22.

He points to the left, where two Imperial scouts sit on speeder bikes in a clearing just ahead. The speeder bikes are vehicles that hover just above the forest floor. They might not be alone, so whatever you and the Rebels do has to be done quietly. Han and Chewbacca sneak up on them and are about to try to knock them out when Han steps on a twig!

The Imperial soldiers spot Han and Chewie, jump off their bikes, and begin to fight. You are about to rush to their aid when Luke spots two other Imperial scouts, also on speeders. They've seen you, and they race away to report what they've discovered! The whole mission will be blown if they aren't stopped!

Fortunately, the pair of speeder bikes abandoned by the first two scouts are still there. Luke and Leia sprint for the bikes to go after the two scouts who got away. There's room for you on the back of one of the bikes, but you don't know if it's right to abandon Han and the others before your mission is completed.

IF YOU DECIDE TO STAY WITH HAN AND CHEWBACCA, TURN TO PAGE 42.

IF YOU DECIDE TO GO WITH LUKE AND LEIA, TURN TO PAGE 47.

You hold it off a few seconds longer. Then you hear a rattling of chains as the palace gate begins to rise. Luke is standing right in front of it, and Jabba's guards are shouting from the other side. You don't want them to see your lightsaber, so you've got to be careful. If this plan doesn't work, you'll need it as a secret weapon later.

The rancor looks up at the opening gate, growls, then takes a step toward it. You stay still, not wanting to draw its attention. The beast starts moving toward the end of the tunnel. Toward Luke.

You are about to scream for Luke to move when he leaps and grabs the opening gate. He is pulled high up with it, out of the rancor's path.

The rancor roars as it lumbers into the palace corridors. The guards scatter, shouting in fear. The palace becomes a hurricane of chaos. People run everywhere, trying to escape the rancor. Several guards and some of Jabba's slaves are slashed and tossed aside by the beast.

"Let's move!" Luke says, dropping to the floor of the tunnel.

You hold your lightsaber at your side as you run for the dungeon. It doesn't matter if you're seen with it now.

FIGHT FOR YOUR LIVES ON PAGE 41.

"Thanks for the save," Leia says. "I don't know how much time it's going to buy us, but . . ."

"It'll have to do," you tell her. "If only Lando can get Chewbacca out of here fast, we might still be able to get away."

"This wasn't part of Luke's plan, Lieutenant," Leia tells you.

"Luke's plan?" Han asks. "Where's Luke?"

"Not here, unfortunately," Leia says.

Han wants to know more, but you don't have time to do anything but shoot. The Gamorreans have called in reinforcements, and some of Jabba's other mercenary soldiers are running up a corridor on the other side of the audience chamber.

"Lando better hurry," Leia says grimly.

Then she yelps in pain as a blaster bolt slams into her left arm! You look across to see where the blast came from and just have time to dive across and knock Han down to save him from being killed.

"Boba Fett!" you say.

"Boba Fett?" Han repeats. "Where?"

You lift your blaster and duck around the corner, hoping to get the drop on Boba Fett, but he's already moved.

HOLD YOUR FIRE ON PAGE 6.

You attack fiercely, slashing at Luke with your lightsaber. He defends himself easily. You lunge. Luke spins out of the way, then turns and thrusts his weapon at you. His lightsaber cuts open your side. You cry out in pain and crumple to the ground, staring at Luke in horror as you realize what you were trying to do.

"I'm sorry," you whisper.

"Kill him!" the Emperor demands.

But you refuse to go after Luke again. The Emperor laughs softly and moves to the huge viewport through which you can all see the battle taking place above Endor. The Rebel forces are badly outnumbered.

"You see, young Skywalker? Your fleet is lost. Your companions on Endor's moon will not survive. There is no escape, my young apprentice."

"The battle's not over yet," Luke says defiantly.

"Ah, good, I can feel your anger," the Emperor says. "You have your lightsaber. Use it. Strike me down with all your hatred . . ."

"No," Luke snaps.

"The hour has come for you to join us, Luke," Vader says. He takes a step toward Luke.

HURRY TO PAGE 24.

"To protect me from the Emperor, I was hidden from my father when I was born. So was my sister," he explains.

"Sister?"

"It's Leia," he says. You are amazed to see him smile. "Leia is my sister."

Luke kneels by you. "You know," he says, "that I have only told you this because you are my oldest friend, and with me, the last of the Jedi. You must not speak of these things until I have done so."

You agree. Then you and Luke fly your X-wings off Dagobah. You rendezvous with the Rebel Alliance as they plan an assault on the second Death Star, which is still under construction. It is protected by an energy shield projected from a small moon called Endor. Han will lead a team to Endor to shut down the energy shield, and Lando will lead the attack on the Death Star. Luke has chosen to go with Han. You must decide which team to join.

IF YOU GO TO ENDOR WITH HAN, TURN TO PAGE 5.

IF YOU ATTACK THE DEATH STAR WITH LANDO, TURN TO PAGE 109.

"We've got to play it safe and follow Luke's plan," Lando argues. "If we attack now, even if you do have some Jedi powers, the odds against us are just too high. With Luke here, it might be a different story."

You stare at Lando. You feel a flash of anger, jealous that Luke is a Master and you are still a student of the Force. But you know Lando is right. Luke spent a lot of time making sure every detail was perfectly planned. You and Lando have disguised yourselves as palace guards for a very good reason: if the plan goes wrong, you'll be there to help out.

So you keep silent as the temporarily blinded Han Solo is brought to the dungeon and locked up with Chewbacca. You don't say anything even when Princess Leia is taken away, dressed in one of the slave girls' costumes, and chained at Jabba's side.

That night you can barely sleep.

Early in the morning Bib Fortuna enters the already crowded audience chamber with Luke right behind him. You know that Luke is using Jedi mind control to force Fortuna to do as he says. It is a talent you do not have.

TURN TO PAGE 56.

"We're not all *trying* to get away, slug," you snarl.

Jabba lets out a deep, thunderous laugh. He mumbles something, and you can barely understand that he is giving you one last chance to live, if you tell him where the others have gone.

"You'll have to kill me before I tell you where they are," you say bravely.

Jabba laughs again. Then, instead of answering you, he attacks! You are surprised by how fast the Hutt can move. He must weigh thousands of kilos, but when he slithers toward you, that huge mouth open as if he means to eat you, you feel fear leap into your heart.

"No!" you shout. In the second before Jabba is about to crush you beneath his huge body, you leap high into the air, put your hands on his head, and flip over him to land in the hallway behind.

The hallway is not wide enough for Jabba to turn easily, and by the time he has maneuvered to face you, you have drawn your lightsaber. You turn it on and it sizzles to life, crackling with energy as you face the gigantic Hutt.

FACE THE HUTT ON PAGE 66.

38

"Obi-Wan has taught you well," Vader says, his mechanical breathing loud in the throne room. "But you are unwise to lower your defenses."

Vader attacks, and Luke defends himself, but it's different now. He's fighting like a Jedi, without rage, without hate.

"Your thoughts betray you, Father," Luke says to Vader. "I feel the good in you. You couldn't bring yourself to destroy me before, and I don't think you'll destroy me now."

Vader seems to hesitate. Then he says, "You underestimate the power of the dark side, Luke. If you will not fight, then you will meet your destiny."

"You don't mean that, Father," Luke says.

"Give in to the dark side, Luke. It is the only way you can save your friends," Vader says, and then pauses again. "Yes. Your thoughts betray you. Your feelings for them are strong, especially for . . . your sister!"

"No!" Luke says, alarmed that Vader has discovered the truth about Leia.

"So, you have a twin sister," Vader says. "Obi-Wan was wise to hide her from me. But now his failure is complete. If you will not turn to the dark side, then perhaps your sister will."

TURN TO PAGE 43.

If you could just buy everyone a little more time, you might be able to hold off until Luke arrives. But your quick action before created this nightmare you're in now. And you are certain that even if you give Jabba the information he wants, he will probably still kill you all.

"Great Hutt," you say, "it was my rash action to attack you. I will gladly go into the rancor pit if you will be merciful and spare the lives of my friends. Princess Leia Organa and Lando Calrissian did nothing but try to help free Solo from the carbonite. Punish me, but set them free, I beg you!"

Jabba stares at you a moment, his huge, lazy face expressionless. Then he laughs, and his whole body quivers with the deep rumbling of his amusement. He mutters something in his own language, and this time no one needs C-3PO to translate. Jabba's guards surround you all and push you forward. Jabba's platform moves backward, revealing a trapdoor in the floor.

You peer down, knowing that once you fall, none of you will ever get out.

TURN TO PAGE 78.

You run at the beast, swinging your lightsaber and cutting into its backside. The huge creature abandons Lando and turns to you. You hold your lightsaber up, ready to hold off the rancor's attack by cutting at its huge paws as it attacks. But the thing reaches out and grabs you, lifting you from the ground. The lightsaber falls from your grasp. The rancor starts to crush your chest in its huge fist. There is nothing you can do!

Quickly, you run out of air. Everything begins to go black. You know that your friends don't stand a chance without you, but you can't hold on for long. A moment later, you fall unconscious as the rancor crushes you in its grip.

Soon you all become dinner for the rancor. Only Chewbacca is still alive, a captive in Jabba's dungeon. When Luke arrives he rescues Chewbacca, but he is too late to save the rest of you.

THE END

At the dungeon, you and Luke knock out two guards who have maintained their posts despite the chaos. You slash the controls with your lightsaber, and the doors open. Chewbacca and Han are free! The four of you run for the main audience chamber. Chewie has to help Han, who still cannot see very well. Lando, Leia, and Threepio are in the chamber, and you're not leaving without them.

Down a side corridor, you hear a familiar series of beeps and whistles. It's R2-D2! Everyone is relieved. Now you only have to find the others. Hopefully, Jabba and Boba Fett are busy trying to catch the rancor.

As you come around a corner just before the main audience chamber, you are startled by someone running straight at you. You raise your lightsaber, but before you can swing, you realize who it is.

"Leia!" Luke shouts.

Chewbacca roars. It's Princess Leia and C-3PO.

"Lando broke me free," Leia says. "We're all here, then?"

"All but Lando," Luke answers.

"I'll go back for him," Han says.

"Are you nuts?" you snap. "You can't even see. I'll go back for Lando. The rest of you go ahead."

Luke looks worried, but he nods. "We won't leave without you."

TURN TO PAGE 105.

You stay with the others and help Han knock out the stormtroopers. Han decides to wait for Luke and Leia before proceeding with the mission. After a while, Luke returns.

"Hey, Luke," you say happily. "Glad you made it back. Where's Leia?"

"What?" he asks. "She's not here?"

"We thought she was with you," Han explains.

Quickly, Han and Luke determine that the Rebel commandoes will go forward on their own, and that you will all rendezvous later to complete the mission. You, Han, Luke, and Chewie are going to find Leia. It isn't easy to track her with the droids along, but the forest floor is almost level, so you manage.

Sometime later, you look around an enormous tree and find a totaled speeder bike.

"Over here!" you shout.

A moment later, Luke approaches. He bends down and picks up the helmet Leia was wearing.

"She must still be alive, then," Han says. "It's the only explanation."

"Artoo," Luke says, "can your sensors find her?"

R2-D2 beeps and whistles sadly.

"Chewie?" you suggest, hoping Chewbacca's keen senses can help.

WHERE IS LEIA? GO TO PAGE 72.

"No!" Luke shouts again. This time he attacks Vader, hacking and slashing. "I won't let you hurt her!"

"That's it. Give in to the power of the dark side!" the Emperor cries with a laugh.

Luke presses his attack on Vader, and now you are worried, too. Luke keeps after Vader until Vader stumbles and falls. Luke slashes with his lightsaber and cuts off Vader's hand, just as Vader once chopped off Luke's! You worry that Luke has finally snapped and given in to the lure of the dark side.

Then he stops once more. Turns off his lightsaber.

"I'll never turn to the dark side," he says, glaring at the Emperor. "You've failed. I am a Jedi, like my father before me."

"And the last of them," the Emperor replies. "So be it . . . Jedi. Since you will not be turned, young Skywalker, you will be destroyed!"

Energy crackles from the Emperor's hands and shoots out across the room. Luke screams as the bolts drive him to his knees in horrible pain.

"Young fool!" the Emperor says to Luke. "Only now at the end do you understand your feeble skills are no match for the power of the dark side. Now you pay the price for your lack of vision."

TURN TO PAGE 48.

As you run, you hide the lightsaber inside your shirt. Luke runs in front of you, darting between the huge monster's legs. You follow as quickly as you can, but the rancor notices your retreat. It reaches between its own legs to catch you, but its arms get tangled and it slows to recover. Its anger may have bought you the time you need to survive.

Luke runs ahead of you. He's always been faster, but this is different. His speed is effortless.

You feel the hot breath of the rancor on your back as you run. Its roar behind you is so loud you want to clap your hands to the sides of your head, but you're afraid to do anything that might slow you down. You can't afford to lose a single step.

Ahead, Luke runs through the open gate into the short tunnel and lunges for the control panel, the one that will lift the door leading out to the palace. Then you're in the tunnel too, out of Jabba's sight. You pull your lightsaber from your shirt. It sizzles to life in your hands. You spin around as the rancor is about to grab you and are able to hold it off with a slash to its arm. You see that the monster has a little piece of cloth from your shirt in its claws. Too close, you think.

KEEP THAT RANCOR BACK ON PAGE 31.

"We can't risk it!" you whisper back. "Leia, Han, and Chewie could all die. Time for Plan C!"

Lando sighs. "I've got a bad feeling about this!"

You charge from the shadows, aiming your blaster at the Gamorrean guards.

"Han! Leia! Over here! We've got to get out of here, and I mean now!" you shout. "Lando, go for Chewie. Run!"

Your attack has given Leia time to aim her blaster, and she fires directly at Jabba but misses. She's too focused on getting Han to safety. Still, she fires again, and this time her blaster shot catches Bib Fortuna, Jabba's right-hand man, in the shoulder. Fortuna falls.

One down, but you've still got the Gamorrean guards and Boba Fett to worry about.

"Leia! Who's doing all the shooting?" Han shouts, as she leads the still-blinded Solo into a small alcove.

Jabba's thunderous voice booms something you cannot understand, and C-3PO is too busy shrieking in terror to translate. The firefight continues, and you blast one of the guards.

You fire several times, then run across the room, diving onto the floor to avoid being shot. You roll into the alcove with Leia and Han.

ROLL ON TO PAGE 32.

You don't think you can take on Jabba one-to-one—Hutts are huge, powerful creatures. And you won't do Lando any good if you're dead. On the other hand, you don't want Jabba to go after the others until they've had time to escape.

Your fear nearly overwhelms you, but you know you have to choose. If you run away, Lando and all your friends may end up dead. If you try to fight the Hutt, he will almost certainly beat you. And if you try to lead him in the wrong direction, to give Luke and the others more time to get away, Lando will be left on his own.

There doesn't seem to be any easy choice this time!

IF YOU RUN AWAY,
TURN TO PAGE 18.

IF YOU STAND AND FIGHT JABBA,
TURN TO PAGE 36.

IF YOU TRY TO LEAD JABBA IN THE
WRONG DIRECTION, TURN TO PAGE 51.

"Wait for me!" you shout.

You run after Leia and hop on the back of her speeder bike just as she takes off after Luke, who is racing ahead after the two escaping Imperial scouts. You feel sick to your stomach as Leia pilots the speeder through the trees at incredible speeds.

"Have you ever ridden one of these things before?" you ask anxiously.

"If you don't like my steering, you're welcome to take over!" Leia calls back over her shoulder.

The forest has become a kind of twisted maze. Up, down, and side to side, branches whip past your face. You can barely keep your eyes on the speeder bikes ahead. Suddenly Leia straightens the bike out and pulls up closer to Luke. He begins to fire on one of the scouts' bikes, hitting it with a blaster shot. It spirals out of control and explodes against a tree.

Only one left!

Suddenly blaster cannon shots flash past you from behind!

"What is that?" Leia asks.

You turn to see two more stormtroopers on speeder bikes coming after you. Then you notice that Luke has slowed and is next to you.

HE MUST HAVE A PLAN.

CHECK IT OUT ON PAGE 13.

Luke screams as the Emperor's power lashes out at him again. You try to stand, try to go to him, but you've lost too much blood.

Vader, already badly wounded from his battle with Luke, stands suddenly. You try to keep him from Luke by fighting with your lightsaber, but Vader is too strong and cuts you down. You are shocked to see him lurch toward the Emperor. Luke is groaning in pain, barely conscious as the energy hits him again and again. Suddenly Vader rushes at the Emperor. With powerful arms, he lifts the withered old man from the ground. Though the Emperor turns all his power on his former servant, Darth Vader throws his master down a long, open shaft at the edge of the throne room.

The Emperor shouts his fury as he falls, but then his voice is gone, and you know nobody could survive such a fall. Vader collapses, and Luke rushes to him.

"Father," Luke says. "Can you hear me?"

"Luke," Vader rasps. "Help me take off this mask."

"But . . . you'll die," Luke whispers.

"Just once," Vader says in his harsh voice. "Let me look upon you with my own eyes."

TURN TO PAGE 55.

When your work is all over, you gather together with your friends. Luke wants to go back to Dagobah to see Yoda. The others have to rendezvous with the Rebel Alliance.

IF YOU GO TO DAGOBAH WITH LUKE,
TURN TO PAGE 94.

IF YOU JOIN THE RENDEZVOUS,
TURN TO PAGE 107.

"Not all of us are *trying* to get away, slug," you snarl.

Jabba emits a deep laugh that sends chills down your spine. He says something. You barely understand that he is giving you one last chance to live, if you tell him where the others have gone. You look around and notice how narrow the hallway is. A plan takes shape in your mind.

"You'll have to kill me before I tell you anything."

Jabba laughs again. Then, instead of answering you, he attacks! You are surprised at how fast the huge Hutt can move. Fear leaps into your heart.

"No!" you shout. In the second before Jabba is about to crush you beneath his huge body, you leap high into the air, put your hands on his head, and flip over him to land in the hallway behind.

The hallway is not wide enough for Jabba to turn easily, and he's stuck—just as you planned. Now you have a few precious seconds to run away.

It is easy to leave Jabba in your dust. You turn down a long corridor. In the distance, you hear the rancor shriek. The monster must have finally been defeated, you realize.

TURN TO PAGE 54.

"And you, young Jedi-to-be, how brave of you to accompany your friend into the enemy's lair," the Emperor says. "I may have some use for you, too. We shall see."

"You're gravely mistaken," Luke says confidently. "You will not convert me to the dark side as you did my father. Soon I will die, and you with me."

The Emperor laughs. "You refer to the imminent attack of your Rebel fleet?" the evil man asks. "I assure you we are quite safe here."

"Your overconfidence is your weakness," Luke tells him.

"Your faith in your friends is yours," the Emperor says. He glances at you for a moment before turning back to Luke.

You can hear Vader's harsh breathing next to you.

"Everything proceeds according to my plan," the Emperor says. "Your friends on Endor, your Rebel fleet, all of them move into a trap. It was I who allowed your Alliance to learn about this station and the shield generator on Endor. From this throne room, you will witness the final end of your insignificant Rebellion. Does that make your hate grow? Take your lightsaber. Use it! Strike me down! I am unarmed."

WHAT WILL LUKE DO ON PAGE 67?

Assuming that the creature is going to attack, you shout in alarm and wake Leia. The two of you try to take the furry little creature's spear away, but it pokes you again. You shout at it, trying to scare it, and it finally turns and runs. You chase it a bit, just to make sure it stays away.

Unfortunately, you have just attacked an Ewok, a member of a race of creatures who live on Endor. The moon is their home. Your attack is considered a declaration of war, and the Ewok you frightened spreads the word among its people. It isn't long before Ewoks swarm over you and Leia and take you hostage.

You are kept prisoner in the Ewok village where Luke, Han, and the rest of your crew soon join you. Unfortunately, you are unable to complete your mission. The Rebel fleet is destroyed because the shield stayed in place, and the Death Star becomes fully operational, solidifying the Empire's hold on the galaxy.

THE END

Jabba is so angry that he does exactly what you hoped he would do. He chases you, which buys time for Luke and the others to get away. If Lando is still free inside the palace somewhere, this may give him the opportunity to get away as well.

"Come on, slug! You'll never catch me! I'll be out of the palace and halfway to Mos Eisley before you can even catch your breath!" you shout to Jabba, spurring him on.

In his thunderous voice, Jabba calls for guards to help capture you, but the guards must be busy elsewhere, because no one responds. The corridor turns left . . . you follow it around and around. You and Lando have been pretending to be Jabba's guards for days now, but you still don't know the palace very well. Especially since you've never run through its halls in the middle of a rancor's attack and a breakout from the dungeon. It's pretty confusing.

Suddenly you round another corner and find your way blocked by a group of palace guards. You stop so fast you nearly fall over. You are about to turn and run the other way when a deep voice growls, "Don't make a move."

You look up and see battered green armor. It's Boba Fett. His weapon is pointed right at you.

UH-OH! TURN TO PAGE 64.

Sadly, Luke removes his father's helmet. You see how scarred his true face is. Still, the strength and honor of the Jedi shines in his eyes.

"There, that's good," Vader whispers. "Now go, my son. Leave me while there's still time to save yourself."

"No!" Luke says. "We're taking the Emperor's shuttle. All of us. I have to save you."

"You have saved me, Luke," Vader says. "Tell your sister . . . you were right about me."

"Father . . . I won't leave you."

"I'm proud that you've grown into the man I once wanted to be," Vader says.

Then, quietly, overcome by his injuries, the man who was once Anakin Skywalker dies in the arms of his son.

A short time later, Luke walks over to where you are lying on the floor, bleeding badly.

"I'm sorry," you tell him.

"I know," he says. "I understand. And I forgive you."

GO TO PAGE 17.

Bib Fortuna approaches Jabba and whispers to him. Jabba notices Luke and shouts angrily at Bib Fortuna in his own language.

"Master Luke!" C-3PO shouts excitedly. "Master Luke has finally come to rescue me!"

"Luke!" Leia calls to him. "Watch yourself!"

Jabba shouts at Threepio, and though you can't understand the words, he is obviously angry and wants the droid to translate. Luke seems very calm. He is a powerful presence in his long black robe and hood.

"The preponderant Jabba gave orders not to admit Skywalker," Threepio announces, and Jabba's anger is clearly directed at Bib Fortuna, who led Luke directly to Jabba.

"I must be allowed to speak, Jabba," Luke says.

Jabba rumbles something at Bib Fortuna, and though the words were probably meant only for Fortuna, Threepio translates: "Weak-minded fools. Skywalker is using an old Jedi mind trick."

"Jabba!" Luke snaps. You know he is trying to control Jabba's mind with his Jedi powers. "Bring me Captain Solo and the Wookiee."

CAN THIS WORK ON PAGE 16?

R2-D2 beeps angrily, and you laugh. Then you can't hear them anymore. The sounds of battle deeper inside the palace echo down the halls. The rancor is still fighting, but you know the battle will not last long. If enough of Jabba's slaves and guards fire at the monster, it will die. You hope the rancor lives long enough for you to find Lando.

The main audience chamber is up ahead. You are about to enter when a huge shadow falls on the wall. You look up and find yourself face-to-face with the giant slug criminal himself, Jabba the Hutt!

Jabba sees you and starts to thunder in his babbling language. Without C-3PO to translate, you shouldn't be able to understand, but somehow you do. Maybe it's your Jedi powers. You know Jabba has just shouted, "Get him, you fools! And find his friends. They're all getting away!"

BE BRAVE AGAINST THE HUTT ON PAGE 46.

"This is all a misunderstanding!" Leia protests, but the Ewoks don't listen.

"Threepio," Luke says quickly, as the Ewoks stoke the fire under Han, "tell them if they don't do as you command and free us, you'll become angry and use your magic!"

"But Master Luke, what magic?" Threepio asks, frantic. "I couldn't possibly—"

"Just tell them," Luke interrupts.

Threepio begins to speak to the Ewoks, but they aren't listening. Suddenly Threepio begins to float off the ground in his chair. You realize that Luke is using the Force to levitate him! The Ewoks are terrified and set Han free.

"Great job, Luke," you whisper.

"Thank Threepio," Luke replies. "He went against his programming and impersonated a deity!"

Later, at a gathering of the Ewok tribe, Threepio tells your hosts the story of the war between the Rebellion and the Empire. You are all made honorary members of the Ewok tribe. They share your fear of the Empire and want to help in your mission and your battle.

But first, there is a feast.

"As long as I'm not the main course," Han says with a laugh.

EAT YOUR FILL ON PAGE 23.

You reach inside your shirt and pull out your lightsaber. With the flick of a switch, it crackles into electric life, humming with power. The rancor darts toward you, and you slash at its clawed hand. The beast howls in anger and pain.

"Now you've done it," Luke says.

And he's right. The rancor's skin is barely slashed, but it's much angrier than before. Fortunately, you are under an outcropping where the people in Jabba's audience chamber cannot see you, so the Hutt doesn't know you are a Jedi with a lightsaber.

Luke glances over at the raised gate used to let the rancor into the pit. Beyond the open gate is a second, closed door.

"If we can get in there and close that gate, we'll be safe," Luke says.

"Yeah," you agree, "but if we can set this guy free somehow, we might be able to use the chaos to grab the others from the dungeon and make a run for it."

Luke looks at you.

"That's pretty risky," he says.

"No more so than your plan," you tell him.

"Hey," you say with a shrug, "look around, old friend. What do we have to lose? Let's set this monster free!"

TURN TO PAGE 70.

"Wow," Lando replies. "Han said it was big, but this thing is huge."

"Just be glad it isn't finished and the weapons aren't on-line yet," you tell him.

"Great," Lando says. "I feel much better."

Lando begins to give orders to the commanders of the other squadrons while you watch the scanners.

"Lando, look at this," you say. "I can't tell if the shield is still up or if Han and the others have already shut it down."

"What do you mean, you can't tell?" Lando demands. "That's impossible unless we're being jammed, and how could they be jamming us if they don't know . . . we're coming . . ."

You stare at Lando. "It's a trap," you say.

"Assault Wing, break off the attack!" Lando shouts.

Suddenly the fleet is attacked by dozens of TIE fighters, the Empire's one-crew starfighters. You also see at least half a dozen Imperial Star Destroyers—huge ships that could do much more damage—waiting in the wings without attacking.

"Why aren't those Destroyers coming after us?" Lando shouts.

GOOD QUESTION. TURN TO PAGE 104 TO FIND OUT.

The audience chamber grows more crowded, the band plays loud music, and the slave girls dance for Jabba the Hutt, their master. When one of the dancers stumbles, she is dragged across the floor into a pit. A huge, monstrous creature called a rancor attacks her. Her screams are so pitiful you almost reveal your true identity and try to save her. But if you did, your whole plan would be off, and more than likely, you and all your friends would join Han as Jabba's captives. You can't take that risk.

Suddenly, amidst the throngs of criminals and slaves, weapon fire sounds over the blaring music. An angry Jabba demands to know who has dared fire a weapon inside his home. A bounty hunter named Boushh pushes forward—leading Chewbacca in chains! Boushh wants to collect the bounty on Chewie! Right on schedule.

"It can't be much longer," Lando whispers to you.

With Threepio interpreting, Jabba and Boushh negotiate payment for Chewbacca, and soon the Wookiee is led off to the dungeons while Boushh joins the nonstop party in the audience chamber.

FLIP TO PAGE 87.

"Told ya, kid!" Han shouts.

You pull your lightsaber, which had been hidden inside your clothes, and face Jabba's guards and soldiers. But their numbers are overwhelming. It isn't long before you are all overcome. In the end, you are all recaptured. But you are set free on the Tatooine desert, while Han and the others are imprisoned.

You are ashamed of yourself. You should have listened to Han and Leia. When you eventually find Luke, you tell him everything that happened and offer to help him break in and rescue your friends. Luke is angry and turns down your offer of help. Thanks to you, Jabba must have been ready. You never again see any of your friends.

For the rest of your life, you must live with what you've done.

THE END

"You're pretty quick on your feet," Fett says.

You can hear Jabba bellowing as he slithers through the hall behind you, getting closer.

"Too bad Jabba's going to want to mount your head on the wall of his audience chamber like a trophy," Fett says, "for letting Solo get away."

"As long as the others escaped—" you start to say.

Jabba's roar of anger interrupts you. He shouts in his ugly language, and you get the basic idea of what he is saying. He is ordering Boba Fett to kill you.

"For what you pay me," Fett says, "no problem."

You're about to defend yourself when Boba Fett pauses.

"On the other hand," he says, "the one you really want is Solo, right?"

Jabba nods in agreement. Fett turns to you.

"How about it, kid?" he says. "I can kill you now, or you can help me recapture Solo. If we get him back, then you get to live. Is it a deal?"

IF YOU DECIDE TO HELP BOBA FETT, AT LEAST FOR NOW, TURN TO PAGE 69.

IF YOU DECIDE TO FIGHT, DESPITE THE ODDS, TURN TO PAGE 82.

As you, Leia, and Han try to break into the base to plant the explosives, Leia is winged by a blaster shot. The stormtroopers move in, and you and Han must lower your weapons. But since you are blocking their view of the wounded Leia, the Imperials can't see that she still has her blaster. When the stormtroopers lower their guard, you and Han leap aside and Leia blasts them.

"That's it—let's go!" you cry.

"Maybe not," Han says.

You look up to see what he's staring at. An Imperial walker has just arrived, its guns pointing right at you and your friends. Suddenly the hatch on top opens. Chewbacca pops his head out and howls a greeting.

It isn't long before the Imperial walkers and other vehicles are destroyed by Ewok booby traps and the Imperial soldiers defeated in the forest. A short time later, you and your friends plant explosives and blow up the base, destroying the shield generator.

HOORAY! TURN TO PAGE 15.

"Luke Skywalker isn't the last Jedi after all," you tell Jabba. "There is at least one more. And while I'm nowhere near as powerful as Luke, I have enough faith in the Force to know that beating you won't be any problem at all."

Jabba only laughs and comes at you again. This time you are ready for him. You swing your lightsaber and slash his body, but he keeps advancing. You attack several times, barely escaping the Hutt's crushing blows. Finally, Jabba falls, but you can't move out of the way in time. Your legs are trapped beneath his great weight. You're lucky they haven't been broken, but now you have to figure out how to get free.

You focus your mind on the Force, trying to use its power to lift Jabba off you. But he is too heavy to levitate. After a short time, however, you realize that if you can lift him just a tiny bit, instead of trying to move him completely away, you may be able to pull your legs out from under him. You focus. It works!

YAY! TURN TO PAGE 28.

"No!" Luke cries. "Never. I'll never give in to hate and fear."

"Give in to your rage!" the Emperor says. "It is unavoidable. With each passing moment, you make yourself more my servant. It is your destiny. Like your father, you will be mine!"

You can feel the rage building in you, and you know it must be affecting Luke. You're tempted to reach for your own lightsaber and kill the Emperor. He must be stopped.

Suddenly the Emperor looks at you and smiles.

"There is another way," he says. "A way that you may serve me, come to the dark side, and I will allow your fleet to escape, and your friends on Endor as well."

You look up, interested.

"How?" Luke asks.

The Emperor glances at you, then turns back to Luke. "This one is your oldest and truest friend. Take up your lightsaber and murder your friend, take the life of one who loves you. Then you will be mine, but your precious Rebellion will survive to battle me another day."

WILL HE DO IT? FIND OUT ON PAGE 29.

Just as they embrace, deep laughter rumbles across the audience chamber. Familiar laughter. A heavy curtain is drawn aside, and behind it, Jabba the Hutt sits in all his disgusting glory. Threepio, the bounty hunter Boba Fett, and several of Jabba's huge, piglike Gamorrean guards wait in attendance.

Jabba commands his guards to throw Han in the dungeon with Chewie and turn Leia into a slave girl to replace the one he fed to the rancor earlier!

You start forward to stop Jabba's men. But a strong hand clamps down on your shoulder. Lando whispers, "No! If we reveal ourselves now, we won't have a chance against them. If we wait for Luke, maybe we can still get everyone out!"

"But if we don't do something now, Han may die before Luke gets here!" you argue. "Jabba may kill us all!"

IF YOU DECIDE TO WAIT,
TURN TO PAGE 35.

IF YOU DECIDE TO ATTACK NOW,
TURN TO PAGE 45.

You feel the weight of the lightsaber inside your shirt. You are a Jedi now, and you can never turn against your friends. But if you play along with Fett, you'll live to fight another day.

"All right, Fett," you say. "I'll help you capture Han."

Jabba laughs long and deep.

Soon you depart Tatooine as Fett's unwilling ally.

You guide Boba Fett to a system not far from the point where Luke and the others are supposed to rendezvous with the Rebellion. From there, you explain, you'll be able to contact Solo, tell him you need to be picked up, and lure him into a trap. Your idea is that when Han and Chewbacca arrive, you can turn on Fett and capture him instead.

At the appointed location you use the subspace frequency to contact the *Millennium Falcon*. Chewbacca gets a message to Han, and the response arrives soon. They're coming. Hours later, the *Falcon* approaches the moon's surface, where you and Boba Fett wait to ambush Han and Chewbacca. Fett has already said that it's up to Jabba if Han lives or dies. You're supposed to take them both alive.

TURN TO PAGE 88.

Luke nods. "Okay, then. We'll head for that tunnel between the pit gate and the door that leads into the palace. Jabba won't be able to see us. You've got to wait until then to use your lightsaber. If we make it that far, you can hold the rancor off while I get to the control panel for the door. Then we just cross our fingers and hope."

"What do you mean, 'if we make it?' "

Luke smiles. "Nobody lives forever," he says calmly.

"Thanks," you reply. "That's very encouraging."

As Luke begins to answer you, the rancor charges, roaring in fury and trying to slash its talons under the outcropping where you are hiding. You swing your lightsaber around again, cutting into its fingers.

"Next time it comes for us, swing at it once, then stash the lightsaber inside your shirt and we'll both make a run for it," Luke says. "We're only going to get one chance at this."

"Let's make sure we only need one," you reply.

Luke nods.

The rancor howls with pain, hunger, and rage and comes for you again. You cut into its talon with your lightsaber, then click it off.

"Now!" Luke shouts.

RUN TO PAGE 44.

You decide to stay with Han and the others. In the morning, you, Leia, Chewbacca, and Han set off through the forest to meet up with the Rebel commandoes. Together, you and your friends, the Rebel commandoes, and dozens of Ewoks sneak in and surround the base housing the shield generator. You hide behind a fallen log with Han, Leia, and several of the Ewoks.

"There's only a few guards," Han says. "This shouldn't be too much trouble."

"The Ewoks were right," Leia adds. "This rear entrance isn't nearly as well guarded as the main door."

"Yeah," you agree, "but it would still be best if none of them got away to warn their buddies."

Before you can go on, Han taps you and points toward the base entrance. One of the Ewoks has slipped out of the woods and mounted an Imperial speeder bike. Though he can't possibly know how to steer it, he manages to get it going just as the stormtroopers notice him. In an instant, he takes off. Most of the stormtroopers follow, leaving only one behind.

"Not bad for a little furball!" Han says. "Get the commandoes into position. Chewie and I will take care of the last guard."

TURN TO PAGE 2.

Chewbacca growls and sets off on a side trail.

"He says he's picked up a scent," Han explains.

Chewie finds the remains of an animal hung from a tree. Artoo beeps and Threepio shakes his head.

"Somebody's lunch? Artoo, what a horrible imagination you have," the droid says.

Everyone moves closer, trying to figure out what any of this could have to do with Leia's disappearance. Something seems very wrong.

"Wait," Luke says, just as Chewie reaches out to touch the carcass. "Chewie, don't touch it! Don't . . ."

But before Luke can stop Chewbacca, the trap is sprung. You, Han, Chewie, Luke, and the droids are caught in an enormous net.

"Nice work, Chewie," Han says. "Always thinking with your stomach."

Luckily, R2-D2 has a small buzz saw inside his squat body, and he cuts you all loose. But your luck doesn't last. As soon as you are free, you are surrounded by dozens of short, furry creatures with spears and clubs. They are set to attack until they see C-3PO. They chatter excitedly, pointing at him.

FIND OUT WHO THESE CREATURES ARE ON PAGE 90.

"Luke, watch out!" you shout. "You're standing on a trapdoor! There's a rancor pit down there!"

Luke reaches out with the Force and grabs a blaster from the hand of a Gamorrean guard. Almost at the same moment, a second Gamorrean grabs Luke around the chest and begins to crush him.

"No!" you shout. You rush forward, pulling your blaster, ready to shoot the Gamorreans.

You fire at one of them, and he goes down, but before you can shoot the one holding Luke in place over the rancor pit, Boba Fett blasts your blaster from your hand! Enraged, you turn and face him, ready to attack with your bare hands if necessary.

"Stand right there or all your friends will die," Fett warns.

You have no choice. You shout another warning to Luke, but even as you cry out, the trapdoor opens, and Luke and the Gamorrean guard both fall into the pit. As Luke faces his fate below, Jabba orders his men to search the palace. Where there is one spy, he cries, there may well be another. It isn't long before Lando is discovered.

OH NO! TURN TO PAGE 101.

"On Cloud City, when I fought Vader . . . when I lost my hand," he tells you. "He said he was my father."

"Told you did he?" Yoda says, shaking his head. "Unexpected this is, and unfortunate."

You stare at Yoda, finding this news almost impossible to believe.

"Unfortunate that I know the truth?" Luke asks, a little angry.

"Unfortunate that you rushed to face him with your training incomplete. Not ready for the burden were you. Whatever the future brings now, remember. A Jedi's strength flows from the Force. But beware: anger, fear, the dark side they are. Once you start down the dark path, forever will it dominate your destiny."

Yoda closes his eyes once more, and his head begins to tilt to one side. He is dying.

"Master Yoda, please . . . ," you say.

"Do not . . . do not underestimate the powers of the Emperor, or suffer your father's fate you will, Luke," Yoda whispers. His eyes open one last time, and he looks at both of you. "When gone am I, the last of the Jedi will you be."

TURN TO PAGE 103.

But it is too late. Luke lifts a hand, and his own lightsaber flies into it. He attacks Vader viciously. Luke is so fast and so brutal that Vader doesn't stand a chance. Quickly, Luke kills Vader.

"Excellent!" the Emperor says. "Now you will take his place."

"No!" Luke screams, and rushes at the Emperor.

Energy crackles from the Emperor's hands, and bolts of power shoot across the room at Luke.

With his lightsaber, he deflects the Emperor's bolts. Luke has given in to his anger and is completely taken over by the dark side. With incredible power, Luke slashes at the Emperor and drives him back to a large, open shaft at one end of the throne room. The Emperor falls into the shaft and screams his rage all the way down. You know nobody could survive such a fall.

"Luke! You did it!" you cry. "You saved the Rebellion! The Emperor is destroyed. If Han can shut down the shield generator, the Death Star will be destroyed as well. Let's get out of here before we're blown up along with it."

But Luke won't budge.

"Luke, come on, or we're dead men!" you shout at him.

HURRY LUKE! GO TO PAGE 81.

Boba Fett leaps out of the way of your next lightsaber attack. By then Jabba's guards have realized that they are in danger from you. They put their arguments aside and try to shoot you down. The lightsaber flashes in your hands, and you deflect their blasts. You rush the guards, who turn and run, convinced they won't be able to beat you.

Which is a good thing, since you are already exhausted and can't keep up this pace a moment longer. You turn to face Boba Fett, but you're too late. Fett has picked up one of the fallen guard's blasters and is pointing it at you.

"You should have taken my offer, kid," Fett says. "Now drop the lightsaber."

You can't do that. The lightsaber is your last chance.

You drop to the floor, roll, and leap to your feet, lightsaber ready once again. But you're not quite fast enough. Boba Fett gives several blaster shots, two of which hit you directly in the chest.

You sink to the floor of the corridor. The last thing you hear is a peal of laughter from Jabba the Hutt. When you wake, you are in the Hutt's dungeon, where you remain for the rest of your days.

THE END

"No!" you shout, and pull your lightsaber from inside your shirt. "By the power of the Force, I will not allow it!"

You swing the lightsaber, and some of the guards do move back. You rush at a big, piglike Gamorrean. But even as you attack, other guards move in on your friends. Leia and Lando are weaponless, and Han is nearly blind. In seconds, they are forced to the edge of the pit and fall in, crying out in alarm.

"No!" you shout. You realize that by attacking, you left your friends open to the assault of Jabba's other men.

Threepio shrieks in distress, but you ignore him. You ignore everything but the roar of the rancor from the pit. You swing your lightsaber at the Gamorreans one last time, then run to the edge of the pit and leap in after your friends.

The rancor has already clawed at Lando, who lies wounded on the floor of the pit. The huge creature has massive fangs and huge fists that could cover you completely. Leia has managed to squeeze herself and Han under a small arch inside the pit, but it won't take the rancor long to get at them. Unless you distract it.

HURRY TO HELP ON PAGE 40.

"Make it two," Leia says. "I'm not letting you out of my sight again."

As Threepio tells Leia that he plans to go as well, because it's what Luke would want, Luke himself enters the room.

"I'm with you, too!" he says.

The room is filled with noise as everyone welcomes Luke back. But you can see he's troubled.

"Luke, what is it?" you ask.

"Later, old friend," he says. "I'll have time to explain it all. I have a lot to tell Leia as well."

"What about you, kid?" Han asks you. "You coming on our suicide mission, or you gonna play it safe and fly into a Death Star with Lando?"

You know Han is only joking. Lando's mission is only a little less dangerous than his. You want to go with them, but your skills as a pilot might be needed.

"I could use you," Lando says.

"So could we," says Han.

**IF YOU GO WITH HAN,
TURN TO PAGE 5.**

**IF YOU GO WITH LANDO,
TURN TO PAGE 109.**

A short time later, Luke joins you all in the dungeon. It is a happy reunion, despite the horrible future that awaits you.

"Luke, I'm sorry," you say. "I really blew it."

"You were just trying to save me," he says. "I appreciate it."

"Don't worry," Leia says. "We'll find a way to get out of this."

Chewbacca roars his agreement.

"I just wish I could see," Han says. "Shapes are starting to come back, and light, but not much else."

Your reunion is cut short when you are all marched back to Jabba's audience chamber.

"How are we doing, Luke?" Han asks.

"The same as always," Luke replies.

"That bad, huh?" Han says with a smile.

Jabba's voice booms in the hall, and Threepio gives a little cry. "Oh dear!" he says. "His High Exaltedness, the great Jabba the Hutt, has decreed that you are to be terminated immediately!"

"Good," Han says. "I hate long waits."

"You will therefore be taken to the Dune Sea and cast into the Pit of Carkoon, nesting place of the all-powerful Sarlacc," the droid explains.

"That doesn't sound so bad," Lando says.

BET IT GETS WORSE ON PAGE 114.

"Go on," Luke says, sitting on the steps in front of the Emperor's throne. "The Rebellion may still win, but I have lost. I let the dark side consume me. All I want now is power. It is taking every ounce of my will not to betray you now and take the Emperor's place on that throne. Leave me here and I'll be destroyed with the Death Star."

"No!" you shout. "You may have fallen, but you can find your way back. Your father nearly did, at the end. I could sense the struggle in him, and so could you. He was ruled by the dark side for decades, and this has just happened to you. You can overcome it, Luke!"

Luke is silent for a few seconds. Then he stands. "I'll come back with you," he says. "But you've got to make sure the Rebellion keeps me a prisoner until you and Leia determine that the dark side has left me completely."

"I'll do it!" you promise.

You and Luke run for a shuttle. Of course, the Rebellion is successful, and the Death Star is destroyed. It is years before you and Leia finally announce that Luke has defeated the dark side. When that day comes, however, it is one of the happiest of your life.

THE END

You feel the weight of the lightsaber inside your shirt. You are a Jedi now, and you can never turn against your friends. Fett glances up at Jabba for a second, and you reach inside your shirt for the lightsaber.

"Never!" you shout as you draw the lightsaber out. It crackles into life, glowing with sizzling energy.

Everything happens at once.

You deflect Boba Fett's blaster bolts with your lightsaber. The guards behind him start to fire, but you dodge those blasts by diving out of the way. Jabba the Hutt is still in the corridor behind you, however, and when you move, the blaster fire hits the massive crime lord. Jabba is slowed but not stopped.

You deflect another blast by Boba Fett and take advantage of the guards' confusion to move in and launch your own attack. With one swing of your lightsaber, you disarm Boba Fett, who was not prepared for you. He is a better fighter than you are, but he has underestimated your speed with the lightsaber.

TURN TO PAGE 77 AND FIGHT ON.

The battle continues. You quickly eliminate three more TIEs. Then you get a feeling of danger. You look up. A battle-damaged TIE fighter is spinning toward you, out of control! You have seconds to target it, or the impact could destroy the *Falcon!*

You swing around, reach out with the Force—there's no time for computer targeting—and fire! The TIE is destroyed. You breathe a sigh of relief.

"Hey, kid, you down there?" Lando calls from above. "It's getting ugly. I could use you up front."

When you join him in the cockpit, you see what he means. The Rebel forces are being overwhelmed. Then, just when you think that it's over and the Empire has won, Admiral Ackbar announces that the shield is down! Han and the others have done it!

"I knew they'd do it," you tell Lando.

"Red squadron, gold squadron, form on me!" Lando shouts. "We're going in!"

The larger ships remain in the battle, but the *Falcon* leads the starfighters straight through the galactic battlefield and into an access tunnel. It takes some truly difficult flying—you're glad it's Lando at the helm and not you—but he manages to outfly the TIE fighters and get to the core of the Death Star.

HOLD STEADY ON PAGE 115.

"Search your feelings, Father," Luke says. "You can't do this. I feel the conflict within you. Let go of your hate."

But Vader has already made up his mind. "It is too late for me, Son," he says. "I have no choice but to bring you before the Emperor. He will show you the true nature of the Force. He is your master now."

"Then my father is truly dead," Luke says.

The stormtroopers herd you and Luke onto an Imperial shuttle behind Vader. You ride up to the new Death Star in silence. It isn't long before Vader ushers you into the Imperial throne room, where huge windows will allow you to watch the arrival of the Rebel fleet any moment now. The Emperor sits in his throne, a smug, evil smile on his shriveled face, your lightsabers at his feet. Looking at the man, you feel the dark power coming off him in waves. You want to fall to your knees and beg for mercy. But you are a Jedi, and you won't fall so easily.

"Welcome, young Skywalker," the Emperor says. "I have been expecting you. I look forward to completing your training. In time you, too, will call me master, just as your father does."

Then the Emperor looks at you. You look away, unable to face him.

TURN TO PAGE 52.

Boba Fett appears suddenly from within the entryway, his own blaster pointed at Solo. He shouts for Han to drop the weapon.

Once again, you reach out with the Force, but this time, you direct your power at Fett. You take him by surprise. The blaster flies from his hand to your own. You stand up, aiming the weapon at him.

You know he has other weapons, but with you on one side and Han, Chewie, and Leia on his other, he isn't likely to make a foolish move. He surrenders.

You all board the *Falcon* with your prisoner. When you return to the Rebel Alliance, Fett stands trial for kidnapping Han and is imprisoned for life.

"There's another I owe you, kid," Han says.

"Don't mention it," you say. "But, yeah, you do."

Chewbacca barks his laughter and even Han grins at your new confidence. Leia tells you that Luke hasn't rendezvoused with the fleet. Everyone assumes he's headed back to Dagobah. Han adds that you have to hurry back because Chief Counsellor Mon Mothma and Admiral Ackbar are holding a briefing shortly.

TURN TO PAGE 107.

Late that night, after everyone has retired to their chambers, you and Lando hide in the shadows of the audience chamber to make sure that Plan B goes smoothly. Presently, the bounty hunter Boushh enters the chamber and glides across the room to the huge carbonite slab. A light on one edge of the slab beeps and blinks, showing that Han is still alive inside.

Boushh presses a few buttons, and the carbonite begins to melt. Moments later, Han is thawed out and collapses into Boushh's arms. Still, you and Lando don't move. You are there as backup. You can't blow your cover until the last moment.

"No," Boushh says. "Don't try to stand up yet."

"Something's wrong . . . ," Han mumbles. "I can't see."

"You have hibernation sickness," Boushh whispers. "Your eyesight will return in time. Come, we've got to hurry."

"I'm not going anywhere," Han says angrily. "Who are you, anyway?"

Boushh takes off his helmet.

"Someone who loves you very much," *she* says.

"Leia!" Han exclaims.

TURN TO PAGE 68.

The *Falcon* lands on a platform near a deep ore mining facility. The noise from the mining machinery is incredibly loud. Boba Fett is hiding inside the entryway to the landing platform as Han and Chewbacca come down the ramp from their ship.

You stride across the platform to Han with a big smile on your face. He smiles as well. Chewbacca roars a greeting but you can barely hear it over the thumping of the mine. You are surprised to see Leia getting off the ship as well, but she is wearing a blaster, so her presence could help with your plans. Solo would not normally hug you, and when you throw your arms around him to pull him close, you know he'll realize something's wrong.

"Hit me!" you shout in his ear.

"What?" he screams back, trying to be heard.

"Boba Fett is here," you shout, knowing Fett won't hear you over the noise of the machines. "Hit me, then draw your blaster like you mean to kill me!"

Han's eyes widen. He punches you right in the face—hard enough that you wish he hadn't been quite so realistic about it—and you stumble backward and sprawl across the platform.

When you look up, he has pulled his blaster and is about to fire at you.

GET TO PAGE 86.

You look at your friends. Han can barely see, but he stands proudly, with his chin raised. He will never tell Jabba what he knows, even if it costs you all your lives. Leia won't speak up either. She is a brave woman, a Princess, and entrusted with some of the Rebel Alliance's greatest secrets. You know from the little time you've spent with Lando that he'd rather die than be a traitor. He proved as much when he sacrificed his operation at Cloud City to save all your lives.

But if nobody speaks up, you will all die. Still, if you can buy some time, even until the morning, maybe you can hold Jabba off until Luke arrives to follow through on his part of the plan.

"Oh, great and powerful Jabba," you say. "You are kind to offer us this . . . generous choice. But I would ask you to be kinder still. Would it be possible, great Hutt, for your poor prisoners to have until morning to make up their minds?"

Jabba begins to laugh.

"What are you doing, kid?" Han barks. "You can't make deals with the Hutt!"

"No, Han, you don't understand!" Leia whispers, trying to keep Han quiet.

WILL HAN RUIN YOUR PLAN ON PAGE 92?

"Threepio!" Luke says. "Do you understand anything they're saying?"

Threepio quickly tries to communicate with the creatures. Then he turns to you and the others.

"They are a race called Ewoks. This moon is their home. They're using a very primitive dialect, but I do believe they think I am some sort of god."

Artoo beeps and clicks his laughter, and Chewbacca snickers.

"Well, why don't you use your divine influence and get us out of this mess?" Han snaps.

"I beg your pardon, General Solo, but that wouldn't be proper," Threepio replies.

" 'Proper?' " Han growls.

"It's against my programming to impersonate a deity," Threepio explains.

Angry, Han moves toward Threepio. The Ewoks bring their spears up again. Soon you are all taken to the Ewok village, where you find Leia. The Ewoks don't like Han, though, and begin to move him toward a fire pit. Han demands to know what's going on.

"I'm rather embarrassed, General Solo," C-3PO says, "but it appears you are to be the main course at a banquet in my honor."

NO WAY! TURN TO PAGE 58.

Quickly, you and the half-blind Han Solo rush over to help Lando. He is dangling over the sand pit and the open jaws of the Sarlacc. Together, you and Han pull Lando to safety. Soon enough, Luke and Leia swing over to the sand skiff as the sail barge crashes to the desert floor. It seems that Princess Leia has fought Jabba the Hutt by herself and ended up strangling the huge crime lord with the same chains he was using to keep her as his slave.

When the dust dies down, you pick the droids up from the desert surface of Tatooine. They were lucky to escape from the barge. You gather together with your friends to discuss your plans. Luke wants to go back to Dagobah to see Yoda, and the others must rendezvous with the Rebel Alliance.

"What are you going to do?" Luke asks.

**IF YOU GO TO DAGOBAH WITH LUKE,
TURN TO PAGE 94.**

**IF YOU GO TO THE RENDEZVOUS,
TURN TO PAGE 107.**

"Great Jabba," she says. "If you would give us until morning, you would truly prove your wisdom and benevolence. We beg you."

Jabba begins to say something, and C-3PO translates.

"While the majestic Jabba enjoys hearing you beg for your lives," Threepio says, "he knows that you are only trying to postpone your deaths a little while longer. And the . . . oh, no!"

"I hate it when he says that," Lando mutters. "It's always bad news."

"The rancor needs his dinner!" Threepio cries.

The platform upon which Jabba sits begins to move backward, and a trapdoor opens beneath it. You can hear the rancor roar deep inside the pit. You look around at your friends and realize that there is only one thing left for you to do.

"No, Jabba, wait!" you cry. "I will tell you anything you want to know!"

"Kid, no!" Solo snaps.

"What are you doing?" Leia asks, horrified.

"The only thing I can do," you answer.

"You'll betray us all!" Lando says.

"I'm saving all of our lives," you explain.

DON'T THEY UNDERSTAND?

TURN TO PAGE 25.

You set out after Luke right away. You manage to follow his path through the forest by focusing with the Force. Eventually you track him to a small Imperial pad. You rush to catch up to him. He senses your pursuit and turns to face you.

"What are you doing?" he asks angrily.

"Following you," you snap. "I'm not going to let you face Vader alone."

"He's my father," Luke says.

You are silent for a minute, overwhelmed by this fact, then your mind clears.

"Yeah," you reply, "and I'm your best friend. And the only other Jedi left. You'll have a better chance to beat him if I'm with you."

"I believe there is still good in him," Luke says. "I can appeal to that goodness and convince him to turn against the Emperor."

You stare at him in disbelief. Finally, you shrug. "Fine," you say, "but I'm coming along anyway, in case you're wrong."

"No," Luke says. "I need you to stay with Leia, to share your training with her, in case I don't make it back."

GO TO PAGE 102.

You know that the Rebel Alliance needs you, but now, more than ever, you want to see Yoda again. You feel that you are on the verge of becoming a true Jedi Knight, and you hope that with Yoda's help, you will learn the ways of the Force.

Together, you and Luke set your X-wings on course for the Dagobah System. It isn't long before you arrive on that gloomy swamp planet, which always seems dark and foggy. When you find Yoda in his tiny hut, he looks slow and weak.

"He doesn't look good," you whisper.

Together, you and Luke enter. You can smell the rootleaf stew that Yoda is boiling over the fire. It has begun to rain outside, and Yoda moves across the hut painfully, tapping his cane. He is glad to see you, but he seems sad as well.

"Hmm," Master Yoda says, "that face you make, my students. Look I so old to your young eyes?"

"No," Luke says quickly. "Of course not, Master."

You don't answer. Yoda does look old and sick.

"I do, yes!" Yoda says. "Sick have I become. Old and weak. When nine hundred years old you reach, look as good you will not, hmm? Soon I will rest. Yes, forever sleep. Earned it, I have."

TURN TO PAGE 99.

Han shouts, demanding to know what's going on. Chewbacca roars and knocks one of the guards off the skiff into the maw of the Sarlacc below, where he is promptly swallowed by the sand monster. You blast another guard and then free Lando. He unties Han, and escape seems likely until Boba Fett uses his jet pack to fly from the sail barge to the sand skiff.

Fett has been a thorn in your side for a long time. You aim your blaster and are about to fire when Lando pushes you down and charges. Fett turns just in time to avoid Lando and knocks him into the gaping hole. But Lando grabs hold of a cable dangling from the skiff just in time. You know he won't be able to hang on for long, though.

HURRY TO PAGE 112.

"I'm sorry, Lando," you whisper. "Luke's been my best friend since I was little. I can't let him face the rancor by himself. Keep your disguise and stick to the plan. Without you, we'll be in real trouble."

You move away from Lando so nobody will notice that you were together. Then you pull off your disguise, draw your blaster, and charge out into the main audience chamber.

You manage to shoot one of the Gamorrean guards just before you reach the edge of the trap-door. From there, you leap into the rancor pit. You can hear Jabba laughing as you fall.

Luke calls out to you as you land, drop, and roll. You come up with your blaster in hand.

Luke is in a corner, holding the enormous meat-eating monster off with a huge bone. "Blaster fire won't even dent its hide! Stay out of its way!"

With that, Luke runs between the rancor's legs, swatting at its knee with the bone as he passes through. The rancor barely notices as it turns toward you. Luke comes to stand by you.

"You may have just thrown your life away, old friend," he says, out of breath.

"I couldn't let you face this alone," you reply.

FACE THE RANCOR TOGETHER ON PAGE 59.

They are safe. But even as you bounce up on the rubbery cable, you know that you are in great danger. You fall again toward the Sarlacc and swing your lightsaber. But its mouth is too wide. There is nothing to cut. The cable pulls tight again, but the Sarlacc snaps its mouth closed around your waist. Your entire head and upper body are in the dark inside the monster's mouth. The beast pulls on you with its mouth until the cable snaps. You have been swallowed by the Sarlacc!

You know that the others are safe, and your sacrifice is not for nothing. Still, you end up in the belly of the Sarlacc, where you will be digested for one thousand years.

THE END

Yoda climbs onto his padded sleep shelf and begins to close his eyes.

"Master Yoda, you can't die!" you say quickly. "We need you still."

"Twilight is upon me. Soon night must fall. That is the way of all things . . . the way of the Force," Yoda says. "But strong with the Force are you both—a Master someday will you be, Luke. Trained well you have. No more do you require. Already you know that which you need."

You see the pain in Luke's face but also amazement as he realizes what Yoda has said. You feel it, too.

"Then, we are Jedi?" you ask.

Yoda shakes his head. "Continue to train, you will," he says. "Luke know you when a Jedi you are."

"Yes, Master Yoda." You've known all along that Luke would become a Jedi Master. It is his destiny.

"But you, Luke," Yoda says. "Close are you. But not a Jedi yet. One thing remains. Vader. Vader you must confront. Then, only then, a Jedi will you be."

Luke is silent. Yoda begins to close his eyes again.

"Master Yoda," Luke says suddenly, "I must know. Is Darth Vader my father?"

You stare at Luke in horror. How could he think such a thing?

FIND OUT ON PAGE 75.

You decide to wait out the crisis. Luke manages to kill the rancor, and you and Lando are greatly relieved. Though the odds seem stacked against you and your friends, nothing that has happened so far will change Luke's plan.

It isn't long before all your friends are brought before Jabba in the main audience chamber. Han is still partially blind, but Luke and Chewbacca help him. Leia is chained to the platform where Jabba's massive bulk rests, and C-3PO is still his interpreter.

"How are we doing, Luke?" Han asks.

"The same as always," Luke replies.

"That bad, huh?" Han says with a smile.

You and Lando hold your positions, waiting for the right moment. Jabba's voice booms in the hall, and Threepio gives a little cry.

"That can't be good news," you mutter to Lando.

"Oh dear!" Threepio says. "His High Exaltedness, the great Jabba the Hutt, has decreed that you are to be terminated immediately!"

"Good," Han says. "I hate long waits."

"You will therefore be taken to the Dune Sea and cast into the Pit of Carkoon, nesting place of the all-powerful Sarlacc," the droid explains.

"That doesn't sound so bad," Han says.

THINK IT GETS WORSE ON PAGE 108?

Jabba's guards hold you and Lando near the rancor pit. The Hutt wants you to see Luke die. But things don't work out the way Jabba would like. Luke grabs a huge length of bone from the floor of the pit. When the rancor lifts him up to chomp on him, he sticks the bone into the beast's mouth, wedging its jaws open! The rancor drops him, and Luke runs for the exit even as the rancor shatters the huge bone between its mighty teeth.

Luke runs beneath the raised exit gate into a short tunnel, but the other end of the tunnel is blocked by a second gate. He is trapped, but he thinks quickly and uses the controls to bring down the first gate right on top of the charging rancor! The beast is killed.

For the moment, at least, Luke is safe! But even so, your cover is blown, and Leia is a slave. How are you all going to get out of this one?

GOOD QUESTION. CHECK OUT PAGE 80.

Before you can respond, a strong light beams down on both of you, and a voice calls out: "Halt! Both of you freeze right there!"

It is an Imperial stormtrooper—a whole group of them, in fact—and you and Luke are captured. The stormtroopers question you and take your lightsabers, but you tell them only that you and Luke are Rebel soldiers alone on Endor. The Imperial troops take you both to the landing pad where Darth Vader is waiting as though he knew Luke was coming. You realize that, through the Force, he probably *did* know.

"Lord Vader," a stormtrooper says, "we found these Rebels at the forest perimeter. They deny it, but I believe there are more of them. I request permission to do a thorough search of the area."

The stormtrooper hands Vader your lightsabers. "They were both armed with these."

"Permission granted, Commander," Vader says. "Conduct your search and bring their companions to me."

The Commander leaves you and Luke alone with Vader and another pair of stormtroopers, who remain silent at all times. Vader looks at you for a moment, then turns to Luke.

BE BRAVE ON PAGE 19.

His eyes close again, but Yoda continues to speak. "Luke, the Force runs strong in your family. Pass on what you have learned. Hear me you must, Luke. There is . . . another Sky . . ."

Yoda's breath slips away, and he speaks one last word: "Skywalker."

Then he is gone.

You sit with Yoda while Luke goes out of the hut. The sadness is terrible, but you know that Yoda is at peace. A short time later, when Luke returns, he has an incredible story to tell. In the swamp, he saw the spirit of Ben Kenobi, and Ben spoke to him.

"Did he say why he never told you Vader was your father?" you ask.

"He said that once my father went to the dark side, he wasn't really Anakin Skywalker anymore. He said my father is twisted and evil. But I believe there is still good in him," Luke says sadly.

"I'm sure there is," you say. "But you'll still have to fight him again, won't you?"

Luke nods. "Ben said that if I don't, then the Emperor has already won," he tells you. "It's my destiny. He also told me what Yoda was saying at the end, about another Skywalker."

ANOTHER SKYWALKER?
LEARN MORE ON PAGE 34.

Before you can answer, the Death Star fires, destroying a Rebel cruiser. The Death Star's weapon systems are operational after all! Admiral Ackbar, the fleet's supreme military commander, orders the fleet to withdraw.

"We won't get another chance at that battle station, Admiral," Lando tells Ackbar over the comm system. "Hang in there. Han will have that deflector shield down in time."

"He'd better," you say.

The Rebel fleet doesn't withdraw. Instead, they keep fighting. But every second the losses continue to add up. If Han, Luke, and Leia don't get the shield down soon, you think, there won't be any more Rebel fleet.

"I'm going down into the belly turret," you announce. "At least I'll feel like I'm doing something."

You move back through the *Falcon*, then drop down into the weapons turret, relieving the soldier who's been firing on the enemy from there. Once you've settled in, you reach out with the Force, targeting the TIE fighters as they swoop past the ship. You zero in on one and blast it right away!

GOOD SHOT! TURN TO PAGE 83.

"If I can't make it back, you have to go without me," you insist.

"How will we know if you're going to make it or not?" Han asks angrily.

Chewbacca roars in agreement.

"Indeed," Threepio chimes in. "We cannot simply take off without you, Lieutenant. It would be unthinkable. Why, we could never show our faces among the Rebel Alliance again if we . . ."

"Luke will know," you say. "Won't you, Luke?"

"I'll know," Luke admits. "May the Force be with you."

"May the Force be with you," you say to all of them.

You turn and begin to make your way toward the main audience chamber. Behind you, Chewie roars one last time, and Artoo whoops off a series of loud beeps. Then your friends turn and head the other way, toward the waiting landspeeder and their escape.

"Well, this is a relief, Artoo," you hear Threepio say as they disappear down the corridor behind you. "Thank goodness Master Luke found you. You simply can't get along on your own."

TURN TO PAGE 57.

You stay to help Han and Lando. They have slid farther down the cable. Han is lower than Lando, and he hangs on tightly, his legs dangling above the Sarlacc's mouth. It is trying to pull him in with a long, powerful tentacle. Chewbacca is trying to haul the cable up, but the two men are heavy, and the Sarlacc is pulling at the other end. You know you have to save them.

"Keep pulling, Chewie!" you cry.

You glance around the skiff and see another cable, this one attached to an anchor. You slice off the anchor with your lightsaber, then wrap the rubbery, elastic cable around your ankles, tying it tight.

You run to the edge of the skiff and dive—right into the mouth of the Sarlacc. With your lightsaber burning bright, you fall down, down into the pit. Han has been pulled down into the sand by the Sarlacc and is covered up to his waist, but you know that he won't actually be hurt unless he gets into the Sarlacc's stomach. You shout for Chewie to yank hard on the cable, pulling Han up from the sand a bit.

The cable reaches its full length and stretches slightly. You swing your lightsaber and slice into the tentacle of the Sarlacc. It bellows in pain, releasing Han. Chewie quickly hauls Han and Lando up.

TURN TO PAGE 98.

You go with Leia, Han, Lando, Chewbacca, and C-3PO to rendezvous with the rest of the Rebel fleet. Not long after your arrival, a huge meeting is called on the Rebel command ship by the leader of the Alliance, Mon Mothma. You learn that Lando has been made a general, and that he has volunteered to lead the attack on the Death Star!

Mon Mothma outlines the Rebellion's plan. The Emperor's new Death Star is under construction, and its defense systems are not yet operational. It is protected by an energy shield projected from a moon called Endor. Before Lando can lead his attack, a small strike force will have to sneak down to Endor and turn off the energy shield.

"I wonder who they found to pull *that* off?" you say, shaking your head at the risk of the mission.

Then General Madine looks over at Han. "General Solo," he says, "is your strike team ready?"

Han going to lead the strike team!

"Well," Han says, "my squad is ready, but I still need a command crew for the shuttle."

Chewbacca roars. It's obvious that he plans to go.

"Well, it's gonna be rough, pal," Han tells the Wookiee. "I didn't want to speak for you. That's one, anyway."

TURN TO PAGE 79.

"In the belly of the Great Abomination," Threepio says, "you will find a new definition of pain and suffering, as you are slowly digested over a thousand years!"

"No!" Leia gasps.

"On second thought, let's pass on it, huh?" Han says.

Chewbacca roars his agreement.

But Luke only stares at Jabba. "You should have bargained with me," he tells the Hutt. "This is the last mistake you'll ever make."

"Ho, ho, ho," Jabba laughs, and says something to everyone. C-3PO translates: "And so dies the last of the Jedi."

You and Lando are two of the guards ordered to escort Luke, Han, and Chewie onto a sand skiff—a kind of small boat that hovers above the desert of Tatooine—that will take them out to the desert to be fed to the Sarlacc. You feel the weight of your lightsaber inside your disguise. You are prepared to use it. Luke's plan is about to come into play.

BE PREPARED ON PAGE 26.

"I'm no fool," you laugh. "I'll go with Lando's suicide mission. It's a little less suicidal than Han's."

It isn't long before the entire fleet is preparing for the assault. Since Han and the others are traveling to Endor in the stolen Imperial shuttle, you and Lando will be using the *Millennium Falcon* to lead the Rebel attack on the new Death Star. Just before you board the ship, you see Han.

"Good luck, kid," he says. "Don't let Lando hurt my baby."

"I'll take care of the *Falcon*, Han," you promise. "You take care of yourself and the others!"

He gives you a thumbs-up, and it's time to go.

The fleet travels through hyperspace to where it can launch its attack. You don't have any time to chat with Lando; everyone is busy checking scanners and equipment to make sure the attack is a complete surprise to the Empire.

"Assault Wing, this is Gold Leader," Lando says finally. "Prepare to emerge from hyperspace . . . now!"

The entire fleet, dozens and dozens of ships, drops out of hyperspace.

"There it is," you whisper, pointing out the cockpit window. "The new Death Star."

TAKE A LOOK AT THE DEATH STAR ON PAGE 61.

Moments later, you hear the familiar voice of C-3PO and the beeping language spoken by R2-D2 as they enter Jabba's audience chamber. They are led by Bib Fortuna, one of Jabba's highest-ranking men. Fortuna's head is large, with long protrusions like pigtails wrapped around his neck. His hideous face looks almost handsome compared to his boss, though. Jabba sits on a platform, a huge, legless slug of a creature with disgusting habits.

As Bib Fortuna tries to explain to Jabba why the droids are there, Threepio, a protocol droid who knows millions of languages, urges Artoo to play a message stored in his data banks.

Suddenly, a large holographic projection of Luke appears in the air above Artoo. A hush falls over the room, as if Luke's Jedi power can be felt even though Luke himself isn't there. Even Jabba pays attention.

"Greetings, Exalted One," the holoprojection of Luke says. "Allow me to introduce myself. I am Luke Skywalker—Jedi Knight and friend to Captain Solo.

"I know that you are powerful, mighty Jabba, and that your anger with Solo must be equally powerful. I seek an audience with Your Greatness to bargain for Solo's life."

WILL LUKE PULL THIS OFF ON PAGE 20?

Luke hasn't noticed Lando's trouble. He's concentrating on taking the fight to Jabba. With a huge leap and a midair flip, Luke jumps from the skiff to the barge and begins to battle Jabba's soldiers. You look up and notice Leia is using her chains to strangle Jabba, but he is fighting her.

You turn your attention back to the skiff just in time to see Han swing one of the palace guards' spears and smash it against Fett's jet pack. The jet pack erupts and sends Fett flying overboard into the sky and then down into the jaws of the Sarlacc. Han's sight must be coming back!

"Han—get Lando!" you shout, unable to reach the rope fast enough.

Even though he cannot see very well, Han leans over to help Lando. Then he falls in as well! He clings to the cable with Lando, trying not to slip into the pit. Leia is calling for help. Whom do you save?

IF YOU GO TO HELP LEIA,
TURN TO PAGE 10.

IF YOU STAY TO HELP SAVE HAN AND
LANDO, TURN TO PAGE 106.

Han shouts, demanding to know what's going on. You and Lando untie him and Chewie. Escape seems possible until Boba Fett uses his jet pack to fly from the sail barge to the sand skiff.

Fett has been a thorn in your side for a long time. You aim the blaster you've taken from one of the captured guards and are about to fire at Boba Fett when Lando rushes at him. Fett turns just in time to knock Lando off the skiff. Lando grabs hold of a cable dangling from the skiff, but he won't be able to hang on for long. The Sarlacc will have another meal!

Luke hasn't noticed Lando's trouble. He knows he has to take the fight to Jabba. With a huge leap and a midair flip, he jumps from skiff to barge and begins to battle Jabba's soldiers.

You fire your blaster at Boba Fett and wound him, but he is too fast for you. He is about to shoot you when Han swings one of the palace guards' spears and smashes it against Fett's jet pack. The jet pack erupts and sends Fett flying overboard into the side of the sail barge and then down into the jaws of the Sarlacc.

ALL RIGHT! TURN TO PAGE 91.

"In the belly of the Great Abomination," Threepio says, "you will find a new definition of pain, as you are slowly digested over a thousand years!"

"On second thought, let's pass on it, huh?" Han says.

"I'll have to agree with Han," you say loudly.

But Luke only stares at Jabba. "You should have bargained with me," he tells the Hutt. "This is the last mistake you'll ever make."

"Ho, ho, ho," Jabba laughs.

That's when you realize the one advantage you all still have. Jabba doesn't know about your power. Your Jedi skills are weak compared to Luke's but stronger than anything Jabba could anticipate. Now, you think, if you can just find a way to use them.

You are all loaded on a sand skiff while Jabba and his followers gather aboard a much larger hover boat called a sail barge. Boba Fett is with Jabba, and so is Princess Leia, chained and enslaved. C-3PO and R2-D2 are also on the sail barge.

On the sand skiff, it's just you, Lando, Luke, Han, and Chewbacca—along with Jabba's guards. The skiff is almost at the Pit of Carkoon, a huge sucking hole in the desert floor where the Sarlacc dwells, eating anything unlucky enough to fall in.

YUCK! TURN TO PAGE 8.

"Lando, there!" you shout. "The reactor!"

You target the reactor and, at Lando's signal, fire a direct hit!

"Now *go, go, go!*" Lando roars. "When that reactor overloads, this whole place is finished!"

The reactor explodes behind you and fire roars up the access tunnel as Lando pilots the ship toward open space. The fire catches up to the *Falcon* just before you get out, but at the very moment the Death Star explodes, the *Falcon* leaps to hyperspace!

After the Death Star is destroyed, it isn't long before the Imperial fleet is beaten. Later, you and your friends all celebrate on Endor with the Ewoks, a race of furry creatures who live on that small moon. The Empire has been crushed, and the smell of freedom is in the air.

THE END

GET YOUR FREE

 **STAR WARS® TOY**

with purchase of the CHOOSE YOUR OWN

STAR WARS™ ADVENTURE TRILOGY!

LIMITED EDITION 3-D HOLOGRAM COVERS

#1 0-553-48651-9 $4.50/$5.99 Can.

#2 0-553-48652-7 $4.50/$5.99 Can.

#3 0-553-48653-5 $4.50/$5.99 Can.

Toys may vary.

HOW TO GET YOUR FREE
 **STAR WARS TOY**

(A $7.00 VALUE)

SEND:

1. Your actual cash register receipt(s) with the purchase price circled (no photocopies accepted) for the purchases of the three books in the Choose Your Own *Star Wars* Adventure *Trilogy—A New Hope, The Empire Strikes Back,* and *Return of the Jedi.*

2. The original top portion of this ad from all three books.

3. A 3" x 5" index card with your name, complete address, and date of birth.

MAIL TO:

Star Wars Free Toy Offer • c/o MSI
25-15 50th Street • Woodside, NY 11377

RULES:

Open to all persons residing in the U.S. and Canada. Void where prohibited or restricted by law. Please allow 6-8 weeks for your Free Star Wars Toy to arrive. Limit 2 rebates per household. No claims may be submitted by groups, clubs, or organizations. Receipts and proofs of purchase will not be returned. Claims must be submitted by January 31, 1999. Offer good while supplies last.

SPONSORED BY

®, ™, & © 1998
by Lucasfilm Ltd.
All rights reserved.
Used under
authorization.

BFYR 182